Stage Fright

Find out more spooky secrets about

Ghostville Elementary™

Ghostville Elementary™

Stage Fright

by Marcia Thornton Jones
and
Debbie Dadey

illustrated by Jeremy Tugeau
cover illustration by Guy Francis

A
LITTLE APPLE
PAPERBACK

SCHOLASTIC INC.
New York   Toronto   London   Auckland   Sydney
Mexico City   New Delhi   Hong Kong   Buenos Aires

*To Marnie Brooks — a friend who
knows the music of friendship.
And of course, to the real Calliope
and Coco-Mo!*

— MTJ

*For all the soldiers and their
families — may the music of
freedom always play.*

— DD

No part of this publication may be reproduced in whole or in part,
stored in a retrieval system, or transmitted in any form or by
any means, electronic, mechanical, photocopying, recording,
or otherwise, without written permission of the publisher.
For information regarding permission, write to Scholastic Inc.,
Attention: Permissions Department, 557 Broadway, New York, NY 10012.

ISBN 0-439-56001-2

Text copyright © 2003 by Marcia Thornton Jones and Debra S. Dadey.
Illustrations copyright © 2003 by Scholastic Inc.
SCHOLASTIC, LITTLE APPLE, and associated logos are trademarks
and/or registered trademarks of Scholastic Inc.

12 11 10 9 8 7 6 5 4 3 2 1   3 4 5 6 7 8/0

Printed in the U.S.A.   40
First printing, October 2003

Contents

THE LEGEND

Sleepy Hollow Elementary School
Online Newspaper

**This Just In: The basement is alive
with the sound of *weird* music!**

Breaking News: Lots of strange sounds have been creeping up from the basement. Even on the third floor, I could hear the *screeching* and *squeaking* of a really bad band. Maybe the third graders are putting on a musical.

Or maybe the famous basement ghosts are back and in a haunting mood. After all, our school *is* nicknamed Ghostville Elementary. And with a name like that, anything can happen!

Your friendly fifth-grade reporter,
Justin Thyme

1
Play

"I have a brilliant idea," Mr. Morton announced. His third-grade students squirmed in their seats. "I have a wonderful way for us to study history."

Jeff slouched down in his chair and tapped his sneaker on the wooden floor. He didn't find history all that interesting. He didn't understand how history could help him become a famous movie actor and director.

Andrew, the class bully, groaned. "There are no good ideas for studying history," he pointed out as he flicked an eraser at Nina's back. Nina glared at Andrew, but he didn't notice.

The twins, Carla and Darla, on the other hand, liked everything about history *and* school. They shushed Andrew so that Mr. Morton could tell them his plan.

Mr. Morton wiped his glasses on a tissue and beamed at the class. Yes, beamed. Jeff had always wondered how a person could beam and now he knew. Mr. Morton's eyes sparkled with excitement as he told the kids his idea.

"Since our classroom is already decorated to look like an old one-room schoolhouse," Mr. Morton said, "I thought we could put on a play about life on the prairie."

Jeff sat up straight and waved his hand in the air. "Play? Did you say a play?" Jeff knew that many famous movie actors got started by acting in plays.

Mr. Morton nodded. "We can get ideas from the book we're reading."

Jeff waved his hand wildly back and forth. "Can we videotape the whole thing so it will be like a movie?" he asked before Mr. Morton had a chance to call on him.

2

"I don't see why not," Mr. Morton said.

Jeff grinned at his friends, Cassidy and Nina. This history lesson was suddenly getting interesting.

Carla raised her hand. "Our little brother is . . . ," she began.

". . . in the second grade," Darla finished for her.

"Can we invite his class?" they both asked.

Mr. Morton clapped his hands. "Maybe Ms. Finkle will let us use the auditorium so the whole school can be invited." Ms. Finkle was the school's principal.

Andrew groaned again. "Putting on a play about *Old Yeller* sounds like more work than writing a book report," he muttered, kicking the back of Nina's chair. Nina sighed. She sure would be glad when Mr. Morton moved the desks around. Sitting in front of Andrew wasn't fun at all.

Jeff smiled all morning. He grinned all afternoon. When the class lined up to go home, he did a little dance in the aisle. "I'm going to be famous," he said.

Nina giggled and tossed her long, black hair away from her face. "What are you talking about?" she asked.

"I'm going to get the biggest part in our play," he said. "Some filmmaker will see it and want me to star in his new blockbuster movie."

Cassidy rolled her eyes as the rest of the class headed out the back door that led to the playground. Nina, Jeff, and Cassidy were good friends and always hung out together.

"What makes you so sure you're going to get the lead part?" Cassidy asked. "I bet I could be a star, too," she said.

"Don't be silly," Jeff said. "The main part is a boy, so I'm perfect for it."

Cassidy pointed her finger at Jeff's chest. "You may be a boy, but you are definitely NOT perfect."

Nina stepped between her stubborn friends. "You can both be in the play," she said.

Jeff shook his head. "There can only be one star, and I'm it!"

2
Too Many Stars

"Shh," Nina warned her arguing friends. "You'll bring the . . ."

"Ghosts!" Cassidy said with a gulp as a blast of cold wind swirled around the room. Green sparkles floated in the air and slowly formed into see-through bodies.

Ever since they could remember, the kids had heard rumors about the basement of Sleepy Hollow being haunted. After all, their school was nicknamed Ghostville Elementary. The kids always thought the stories were silly, but when their class moved to the basement, Jeff, Nina, and Cassidy found out the stories were more than just rumors. The ghosts were real.

Nina got the shivers as two ghost boys,

two ghost girls, and a ghost dog hovered around her. One ghost girl, Sadie, smiled at Nina. Sadie was usually sad and mopey, but when she smiled, everything about her changed. Her green color turned pink. Her stringy hair bounced with soft curls, and her dark eyes sparkled.

Nina shivered again, but she tried not to dodge the ice-cold touch of Sadie's hand as it passed through her hair. Nina knew Sadie was trying very hard to be a good friend, and Nina didn't want to hurt Sadie's feelings.

One of the ghost boys

named Ozzy walked through a desk toward Jeff. Ozzy didn't even slow down as his body floated through two chairs. "What is all this fussing about?" he asked in a booming voice.

Jeff gulped, and Cassidy squeaked out, "We were just talking about our classroom play."

"I'm going to be the star," Jeff bragged.

"What about me?" Cassidy asked, forgetting all about the ghost glaring down at her.

"Play?" Ozzy asked. His eyes shone like two beams from a flashlight. "I like to play."

"Me, too! Me, too!" Becky sang out. As she jumped up and down her feet sank deep into the floorboards. Becky was Ozzy's little sister. She was younger than the other ghosts and not nearly as good at concentrating on solid things. When she forgot to think hard, she ended up sinking into the floors and walls.

Nate, the other ghost boy, didn't say a

word. He never had much to say. Instead, he turned somersaults through the air above the kids' heads.

Ozzy's ghost dog, Huxley, barked at Nate and tried to nip the seat of his pants as Nate tumbled by.

"This isn't a game," Nina said. "A play is when people act out a story," she explained. "They pretend they are the characters in the story."

"Really good actors are called stars," Jeff said. "And since I know the most about acting, I'm going to be the star of our class play!"

Becky folded her arms over her glittering chest. "We know what a play is. Just because we're ghosts doesn't mean we're stupid."

"Being the star sounds like the best part," Ozzy said. "That's what I want to be."

Becky floated over to sit above Mr. Morton's desk. "I think I could be a star, too," she said. Becky didn't always agree with her ghost brother, Ozzy.

"Listen," Jeff said. "I'm a natural for this play. I already know the story." To prove his point, Jeff jumped up in a chair and started speaking lines from the book. "'But, Mama, you don't mean we'd keep an old ugly dog like that.'"

Ozzy did not like being ignored. He floated behind Jeff and turned as green as a pea.

His ghost friends hovered in the air as if they were an audience watching a great performance. They clapped for Ozzy, but since their hands passed through each other, they didn't make any sounds.

Nina couldn't help but giggle. If the play had been about crazy ghosts, Ozzy would definitely be the star.

Jeff didn't see Ozzy. Jeff snatched the novel from his desk and read from it. "'We can't do without Old Yeller.'"

Ozzy wasn't impressed with Jeff's acting. Ozzy's eyes bulged out until they were the size of baseballs. They dangled from his eye sockets as if they were on a spring. Finally, Ozzy fell to the ground, letting his feet stick straight up in the air for a quick second before flopping down to the floor.

Becky, Sadie, and Nate clapped and

clapped for Ozzy. Huxley barked and licked Ozzy's nose.

The ghosts weren't as nice to Jeff when he finished reading his part. In fact, the ghosts booed. Cassidy thought the booing was sort of odd. After all, they were ghosts. They *should* say "boo." But it was only the second time since Cassidy and her class had moved into the base-

ment that she had ever heard a single *boo* from their resident ghosts — and this time, the *boo* wasn't scary. In fact, it made Cassidy giggle.

"That's not funny," Jeff yelled. "Someday, I'm going to be a great actor."

"I'm already great," Ozzy snapped back.

"I could be better than both of you," Cassidy argued.

"What about me?" Becky wailed and kicked at Ozzy's shin. Of course, her foot went right through her brother's leg.

Cassidy argued with Jeff. Becky and Ozzy yelled at each other. Nate swished through the air. Sadie floated about, moaning softly. Huxley barked at them all.

Nina held up her hand and tried to reason with everyone, but nobody listened. They were all so busy fighting, not a single one heard the door to the classroom slowly creak open.

"Stop!" someone yelled from the hallway.

3
Just an Act

The door swung open and banged against the wall. A tall figure filled the doorway.

"Oops," Becky said with a giggle.

"See you later," Sadie whispered to Nina.

"This isn't over," Ozzy warned.

And with that, the six ghosts disappeared like bubbles popping into thin air. Only Huxley was left. "*Yip, yip,*" Huxley barked as he darted to hide in the back of the room.

Olivia, the school janitor, stepped into the room. Her dangling earrings jingled as she looked to her right. They jangled when she looked to her left. They clunked against the heavy brass buckles

of her overalls when Olivia looked up at the air above the kids' heads.

"I heard voices," Olivia said. "Lots of voices. Who else was in here?"

Jeff, Cassidy, and Nina didn't say a word. Olivia didn't scare them, but the snake wrapped around her neck did. With his head raised to look over Olivia's curls, the snake's tongue darted in their direction. Olivia was always saving animals, but the kids had never seen her with a snake before.

"Why are you carrying a snake?" Nina finally asked. Her voice cracked, and she took a step behind Cassidy. It was a well-known fact that Nina hated creatures with eight legs, but until now, she didn't realize she was also afraid of animals with no legs at all.

Nina wasn't the only one in the room who was scared of Olivia's new pet. Huxley hovered near the back of the room; his ghostly shine had turned a sickly shade of purple. His legs shook and his eyes were crossed as he stared at the snake. Cassidy distinctly heard Huxley whimper.

The snake hissed. It slowly made its way down Olivia's arm and stared straight at Huxley. Huxley hunkered down and tried to hide his nose in his paws.

Cassidy worried that Olivia would see the ghost dog, but then she remembered that no adult had ever seen a Ghostville ghost.

"Don't mind Timothy," Olivia said. "Trying to scare people is all an act. He wouldn't hurt a flea. He's just checking things out. Like me. Now, who belonged to those voices?"

Cassidy glanced at the back of the room where Huxley trembled. "Umm," she stammered. "It was nobody."

"Nobody?" Olivia nearly roared. "Don't be silly. How can voices come from nobody?"

Cassidy did not like being called silly. Someday Cassidy planned on being a computer analyst for the FBI and computer spies definitely were not silly. Cassidy was tempted to tell Olivia that a ghost had *no body*, but Nina spoke up first.

"We were practicing," she fibbed, "for our class play."

"That's it!" Jeff yelled. "Our play. We were trying out our lines using different voices."

"So you're having a play, is that it?" Olivia asked as she gently stroked the smooth scales on Timothy's back.

"And I'm going to be the star," Jeff said, bending low to the ground as though he were bowing to an audience.

"Actually," Cassidy said through clenched teeth, "*I'm* going to be the star."

Olivia looked at them both. "Don't you have to try out for the lead part?"

"Try out?" Jeff asked, standing up straight again.

Olivia nodded. "Auditions are always held so the director of the play can decide who is right for each part. Instead of arguing, you might try helping each other get ready for the tryouts," Olivia said, hoisting Timothy back up to her shoulders. "There's room enough on a stage for everyone to shine. Isn't that right, Timothy?"

Timothy tasted the air in front of Olivia's nose. Then Olivia and her pet snake turned and left the kids alone in the basement of Sleepy Hollow Elementary School.

"That was a close call," Cassidy said as

the three friends grabbed their back-packs to go home.

"Do you think Olivia saw any of the ghosts?" Nina asked.

Jeff shook his head and trotted up the back staircase with his friends. "Thanks to my quick thinking and my acting ability, she thinks we were practicing for the play."

"If you're so smart about acting, why didn't you know about the tryouts?" Cassidy asked, stepping around a pile of dog poop on the sidewalk.

Jeff's face turned red. "I forgot about auditions," he admitted.

"Don't worry," Nina told him. "I bet you'll get the lead part if you practice for it."

"What about me?" Cassidy asked. "Maybe I'm the perfect person for the lead part."

"Remember what Olivia said?" Nina told her. "There are plenty of parts in the play. You and Jeff can both be stars."

"She's right!" Jeff said, perking up as the kids turned down a side street. "We'll both be famous."

"People will ask for our autographs," Cassidy said.

"And we'll have to ride in a limousine to school," Jeff added. "It will be fantastic!"

Jeff and Cassidy were so busy daydreaming that they didn't see the sign beside the sidewalk.

"Look!" Nina said, pulling her friends to a stop. "It can't be!"

4
The Blackburn Estate

A freshly painted sign had been pounded into the dirt at the end of a long driveway that led to the old Blackburn Estate.

"SALE: EVERYTHING MUST GO. TODAY ONLY!" Nina read out loud.

"I didn't know anything was left in that old place," Cassidy said. "No one has lived there since before we were born."

"No one would dare live there now," Jeff said. "At least not according to that old legend."

"What legend?" Nina asked.

Jeff shrugged. "It's just an old story about how all the people who've ever lived there disappeared."

23

"Disappeared?" Nina asked, her voice shaking.

"People moved in," Jeff said, "and then they were never seen or heard from again. They just vanished." When he snapped his fingers, Nina flinched.

"That's just a silly story," Cassidy said.

"Whatever they're selling, it has to be ancient," Jeff said.

"You're right!" Cassidy exclaimed. She slapped Jeff on the back so hard, he had to jump forward to catch his balance. "We have to go to the sale."

"Are you nuts?" Jeff asked. "Why would you want musty old junk from the Blackburn Estate?"

"I don't want anything for me," Cassidy told him, "but since our classroom is decorated to look more than 100 years old, there might be some old stuff at the estate that we could use."

"Great idea!" Nina said.

"We don't have time to go on a shopping spree," Jeff argued. "We have to practice for the play tryouts."

Cassidy patted Jeff on the back again. "You just had another good idea!" Cassidy said. "We can find props for our play, too."

The girls grabbed Jeff's elbows and pulled him up the long driveway. "You won't regret this," Cassidy told him.

"I hope you're right," Jeff said. "Or you'll be sorry."

The Blackburn Estate stood at the end of an old tree-lined gravel drive. Long shadows darkened the way as Nina's, Cassidy's, and Jeff's sneakers crunched the gravel.

The Blackburn Mansion sprawled out like a giant spider's legs. Many windows were boarded over, and loose tiles from the roof flapped in the wind. A tree limb scraped the house, sounding like giant fingernails on a chalkboard.

Jeff grinned. "It looks like a set from one

of my favorite monster movies," he told his friends. "I wish our class play was about scary monsters instead of boring history."

Nina stopped, not wanting to go any farther. "I'm not going into any place that looks like a haunted house from a horror movie," she said. "What if the stories are true, and we never come out?"

"Don't worry," Cassidy said, putting her arm around Nina's shoulders. "We face ghosts every day when we're at school. This will be a piece of cake."

The kids climbed the crumbling steps and made their way across the squeaking boards of the porch. The door stood open, so the kids stepped inside.

The inside of the mansion was just as spooky as the outside. Portraits of people dressed in clothes from long ago hung on the walls.

"It feels like they're watching us," Nina whispered.

Jeff and Cassidy looked at the old paintings. Sure enough, when Jeff stepped

to the right, the eyes in the portraits seemed to follow him. "It's just the way they're painted," Jeff told her, but he didn't sound very sure.

"May I help you?"

Jeff, Cassidy, and Nina jumped at the sound of a voice. In the dimly lit hallway stood a tall woman dressed entirely in gray, from the tips of her pointy shoes to the top of her high-necked sweater. Even her tightly pulled-back hair was gray.

"My name is Thelma B. Hawkins. I am the caretaker of this residence," the woman told them.

"We saw the sign," Cassidy said bravely. "We thought we could find things for our school."

"School?" Mrs. Hawkins asked. "What would a modern-day school want with antiques such as these?"

When the three kids explained how they had decorated their classroom to look like a school from long ago, Mrs. Hawkins' eyes seemed to sparkle.

"That's not all," Jeff said. "We're putting on a play, and we need props to show what life was like in the 1800s."

For the first time since they'd seen her, Mrs. Hawkins smiled. "What a wonderful idea," she said. "Your school sounds like the perfect place for some of my more . . . unusual . . . pieces."

Mrs. Hawkins guided the three kids into the parlor. Her shoes echoed against the hardwood floors. The room was filled with furniture, rugs, and pictures, but what Nina, Cassidy, and Jeff really liked were the old musical instruments hanging on the walls. As soon as Mrs. Hawkins noticed how interested they were in an old fiddle, she gently removed it from the wall where it hung.

"Yes," she said. "I believe this would be perfect for your play. After all, fiddles were used to entertain the pioneers. Please, take it."

"We could never afford something like this," Nina said politely.

Mrs. Hawkins nodded. "To be sure. This is an unusual piece, and I dare not let just anybody take it. It needs a special home where it can be, shall we say, truly appreciated. Your classroom sounds like just the place. So, please, take it as a gift from me."

"For free?" Jeff asked.

Mrs. Hawkins smiled and nodded. "For free," she said. "There is one condition, however. You also must take this dish and keep it near the fiddle. Seems like such a silly thing, but the two belong together."

Cassidy took the tiny plate Mrs. Hawkins held out. There was nothing special about it ex-cept for a small chip along the edge. Still, the plate felt cold in her hands, and Cassidy wanted to give it back.

"We'll be sure

to keep them together," Nina said before Cassidy could argue.

"We really shouldn't accept such expensive things," Cassidy said.

"It is too late," Mrs. Hawkins said as she ushered the kids down the hall and out the front door. "These already belong to you. I have a feeling you three will soon understand their true value." And with that Mrs. Hawkins closed the front door to the Blackburn Estate.

When Cassidy paused to look up at the old mansion, a gust of wind blew in her face and ran across the strings of the fiddle in Jeff's hand. Three strange-sounding notes sent shivers down Cassidy's spine. The plate in her hand felt icy and wet.

"Something is wrong," Cassidy told her friends. "Very wrong. Let's get out of here!"

5
Music

"This is spectacular," Mr. Morton said the next day at school. He held up the fiddle to admire.

"We got it from the old Blackburn mansion," Nina told him. "They were having a . . ."

". . . huge clearance sale," Jeff finished for her. "And I bet we could have gotten a lot more free stuff if Cassidy hadn't wanted to leave so quickly."

Cassidy shivered. Something about the fiddle and the little china plate gave her the creeps. She wished they had never gone inside the Blackburn Mansion. She wondered if she could sneak the fiddle and plate back there without getting caught.

The fiddle didn't seem to bother Mr.

Morton at all. In fact, he put it and the plate on a top shelf in the front of the room. "Now, let's get busy practicing our multiplication tables. We're all the way up to the sixes!"

Andrew groaned, but Cassidy kept her eyes on the fiddle. Finally, she had to look away to start copying math problems from the chalkboard. She was trying to remember six times seven when she first heard the strange sound.

Three musical notes filled the air and stayed there for a long time. Immediately,

Cassidy looked at the fiddle, but it was completely still. Cassidy shrugged and wrote the number forty-three on her paper. She shook her head and erased the three to make forty-two.

The sound came again, and Cassidy

snapped her head up. The fiddle still sat on the top shelf. Nobody could reach it, and everyone was seated at their desks. "Nina," Cassidy whispered. "Did you hear that?"

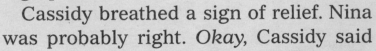

Nina lifted her head up and nodded. "It must be the orchestra practicing upstairs."

Cassidy breathed a sign of relief. Nina was probably right. *Okay*, Cassidy said to herself, *what's six times eight?* She lifted her pencil to write the answer when music suddenly filled the air. It wasn't from the orchestra upstairs. It was definitely coming from inside

their classroom, and it was definitely fiddle music.

Cassidy checked behind Nina. Maybe Andrew had sneaked in a set of headphones and was playing a trick on her. But Andrew wasn't wearing headphones. He was busy flicking spitballs at Carla and Darla.

Several kids did have their heads up though, as if they heard the music, too. Even Mr. Morton was tapping his foot underneath his desk.

"Whew."

Cassidy breathed a sigh of relief. For a minute, she had thought she was going crazy.

All morning long, the kids heard the strange haunting sound of a single fiddle. Finally, when it was time for gym class, the music stopped.

"Thank goodness, that music was driving me crazy," Nina said to her friends. They were standing at the back of the line.

"I liked the music," Jeff said. "It made the time go faster. Now, we can have some fun in gym."

Nina grinned. She loved anything to do with sports.

"Wait a minute," Cassidy said as the rest of the class filed out the door. "I have to show you something."

6
Tryouts

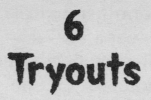

The three kids stared at a shadow near the front of the room. It glittered and glowed for a minute before disappearing completely.

"Did you see that?" Cassidy gasped.

Jeff shrugged. "That's just Ozzy, Becky, Sadie, or Nate."

"Or Edgar," Nina added.

"I don't think it's one of our ghosts. And Edgar is too busy writing ghost stories," Cassidy said, pointing to a picture hanging in the back of the room. The kids knew that Edgar preferred to sit under the tree in the picture and write in his journal. Sure enough, he was there.

"And the rest of the ghosts would pop right up to scare us," she added with a shiver.

"What else could it be?" Nina asked.

Cassidy shook her head. "I don't know, but I don't like it."

"I don't like being late for gym," Jeff said. "Let's go."

Cassidy wondered about the shadow all during the volleyball game and later during free reading and spelling time. Jeff, on the other hand, didn't give the strange shadow a second thought. His mind was centered on the play tryouts that afternoon. His stomach felt queasy just thinking about them. He really wanted to get the main part. He kept saying the lines over and over in his mind.

Finally, at 2:00 in the afternoon, Mr. Morton cleared his throat. "Okay, everyone," he announced. "It's time for the play auditions."

A few kids groaned, but most people cheered. Carla and Darla clapped their hands. Everyone put away their spelling worksheets and took out their copy of the book the class had been reading together.

"Remember, each part is important," Mr. Morton told the class. "And we will need everyone's help to make the set and decorations for the play."

"Now, let's see who is interested in playing Travis?" Mr. Morton asked. Jeff, Andrew, and Cassidy raised their hands in the air.

Andrew glared at Cassidy. "Travis is a boy," he told her.

Cassidy held her head high. "A true actress can perform any part," she said.

Jeff looked at Andrew. "I figured you didn't like plays," Jeff said.

Andrew shrugged. "I thought I'd give it a try."

Andrew went first, and Jeff had to admit that Andrew was pretty good. Cassidy went next and read her part out loud. Jeff sank down in his seat. Cassidy was really good, too. When Mr. Morton called

his name, Jeff walked slowly to the front of the room.

Jeff turned his book to page six and opened his mouth. Nothing came out. Jeff stood frozen to the floor like time had stopped.

"What's wrong with Jeff?" Nina whispered to Cassidy.

Slowly, Cassidy turned to see what Jeff was looking at. "Jeepers, creepers!" Cassidy gasped.

7
Stage Fright

Jeff stared at a strange figure hovering in the back corner of the room. It was a girl dressed in a flowing white gown. Her long, dark braid floated above her head as she bowed slightly to Jeff.

Of course, only Jeff, Cassidy, and Nina could see her. The rest of the class, including their teacher, didn't realize a new ghost was in their midst.

"Jeff? Jeff?" Mr. Morton asked. "Are you okay?"

Jeff's mouth moved, but no sound came out.

"Look at him," Andrew blurted out. "He's got stage fright."

"It's a fright, all right," Nina murmured. "But it has nothing to do with a stage."

The new ghost slowly floated through the air, straight to the items the kids had brought back from the Blackburn Estate. Her slender, pale fingers ran along the chip on the small dish.

Finally, the strange ghost paused in front of the fiddle and smiled. She gently plucked three strings. They played the same tune Cassidy had heard at the Blackburn Estate. The notes seemed to bounce off the walls as the ghost floated over to hover beside Jeff. Then she tilted her head, closed her eyes, and began to sing.

Her voice was high and loud. A good dose of screeching was mixed in, though it sounded like it came from a different part of the room.

Cassidy looked all around the room to find who or what was doing the screeching. The rest of the kids didn't seem to hear a thing. Well, at least not the rest of the third graders. The other ghosts heard the singing, loud and clear.

Cassidy watched as their shimmering shapes gradually took form. First Ozzy. Then his sister. After Becky came Nate and Edgar. The kids didn't see Edgar too often. It took a lot to get him to leave his comfortable spot where he spent time writing stories in his journal.

Edgar pushed his way to the front of the ghostly gang to get a good look at the new ghost. Ozzy wasn't too happy about being pushed aside. He gave Edgar a shove.

Edgar went tumbling through the air, screeching the entire way.

"No, you don't," Becky yelled. She floated above her brother to get a better look.

Through it all, the new ghost sang as if she hadn't seen a thing, and the yowling from across the room didn't stop for a minute.

Nina put her fingers in her ears. Cassidy covered her ears with her hands. Jeff stood at the front of the room and stared.

Of course, they were the only kids who saw or heard any of the ghostly antics.

"Jeff, do you still want to try out for the play?" Mr. Morton asked gently. "You don't have to if you don't want to. I can give the part to someone else."

That was enough to snap Jeff out of his stupor. He forgot all about the singing ghost and looked at his teacher. "Of course I want to try out," Jeff said. "I'm perfect for this part."

Jeff tried to ignore the singing. He concentrated on reading Travis' lines for the play. "'Arliss! You get out of that water!'" he began reading.

But the louder the new ghost sang, the louder Jeff had to yell out his part. Soon, he was shouting so the kids in the front row had to cover their ears. Carla and Darla giggled, and Andrew laughed out loud.

"Thank you, Jeff," Mr. Morton finally said. "I think you've shown the rest of the class that you can project your voice so all can hear."

Just then, Huxley floated to the middle of the room and lifted his nose. He let out a howl that Cassidy was sure shook the

walls. It was so loud, in fact, that it broke the ghost sound barrier. Mr. Morton stopped dead in his tracks. Carla and Darla screamed. Cassidy and Nina fell to the ground and hid under their desks.

Mr. Morton wiped chalk dust from his glasses until he had two clear circles to see through. "What was that?" Mr. Morton gasped.

The room had suddenly grown quiet — very quiet. Cassidy, Nina, and Jeff looked around. Jeff saw a tiny shadow huddled on top of the bookshelves.

"Oh, no," Jeff muttered. "It can't be!"

8
Ghost Invasion

The shadow on the bookshelf uncurled and stretched. Then it leaped from the shelf to the top of a desk. The shadow shimmered and glimmered and slowly took shape until it became a black cat with big, yellow eyes. It looked up at Jeff, arched its back, and hissed.

Huxley barked. He followed the cat as it made its way around the room, jumping from a shelf to a desk to a chair and back to a shelf again. Finally, the shadow came to a stop on the shelf that held the tiny chipped plate.

"Is that what I think it is?" Nina whispered to Cassidy as Mr. Morton clapped his hands to get the rest of the class's attention.

Cassidy nodded. "It's a ghost cat," she

said, "and our resident dog doesn't like it one bit."

Jeff made his way back to his seat. He paused long enough to lean over Cassidy's desk. "Did you see that?" he asked.

Cassidy nodded again.

"That ghost ruined my audition," he said.

"We have more to worry about than your part in the play," Cassidy said.

Nina and Jeff looked to the front of the room where Cassidy pointed. The new ghost was perched on top of the shelf, the black cat nestled in her lap. "Where did they come from?" Nina whispered.

"Maybe the girl came in with the

fiddle and the cat came in with the dish,"
Cassidy said. The kids had learned from
a bad experience that ghosts had to stay
with their belongings. "Along with the
fiddle and dish, we brought ghosts."

"More ghosts?" Nina asked. "What if
Ozzy and his ghostly gang don't like
them?"

"I don't think we have to worry about
that," Jeff said. He was right. Ozzy and
Becky were huddled by the new ghost. In
fact, all the ghosts were clustered nearby
to meet her.

"My name is Calliope," the kids heard
her tell the other ghosts. "And this is
Cocomo. I've had no one to sing to but
my kitty-cat in ever so long."

"Now you can sing to us," Ozzy said.

Cassidy couldn't believe her ears.
Neither could Jeff. "Don't tell me Ozzy
likes Calliope," he said. "I mean, really
likes her."

"It does seem as though Ozzy is, well,
in like with the new ghost," Nina said.

"More, more, more," Ozzy chanted every time Calliope stopped singing.

Cocomo, however, did not like Calliope's song. She *yowled* at the sound. "If I were that cat, I would be going loony-tunes, too," Jeff said. "Nobody — not even a ghost — should have to listen to music like that for all of eternity."

Calliope didn't seem to think anything was wrong with her singing. Neither did Ozzy. Ozzy sat with his chin in his hands and watched Calliope sing one song after another. The louder Calliope sang, the more Cocomo hissed and ran. The more Cocomo ran, the more Huxley chased her.

When Mr. Morton turned to write math homework problems on the board, Cocomo dashed across his desk, sending papers fluttering to the floor. Mr. Morton looked at Andrew.

"I didn't do it," Andrew said.

When the class was planting seeds in milk cartons for a science experiment, Huxley chased Cocomo under the table.

"*AAAAHHH!*" Carla screamed.

"*HHHHAAA!*" Darla screamed.

They both jumped up, knocking dirt and seeds on the floor.

Carla pointed beneath the table. "Something is under there," she said.

"Something big," Darla added.

But when Mr. Morton peered under the table, he didn't see anything except a pile of soil. The girls hurried to sweep up the mess, but they weren't very happy about it. The entire time, Calliope sang and sang.

While the twins were cleaning up the dirt, Huxley dived across the back of the room, his jaws nipping Cocomo's tail. Cocomo screeched and jumped on the shelf that held the class' lunches. Lunchboxes crashed to the floor, spilling leftover bologna, bananas, and juice.

"We'll clean it up," Nina offered before Mr. Morton could say a word.

Nina, Cassidy, and Jeff waited until the

bell rang and the rest of their class filed out of the room.

"This has to stop," Nina said. "I can't get any work done."

"I can't think straight," Jeff complained. "It's no wonder my audition was a disaster."

"This is turning into a nightmare," Cassidy said, putting her hands over her ears. "I can't think with all that noise. YOU HAVE TO STOP!" she shouted at Calliope.

The room suddenly went silent as Calliope looked at the three kids. "Stop?" she asked. "But this is the first time in ever so many years that I've had an audience besides my faithful cat. I cannot stop now. I can never stop!"

"More! More! More!" Ozzy chanted.

Cocomo wrapped around Calliope's ankles as Calliope bowed toward Ozzy. When she did, Ozzy handed her the fiddle from the Blackburn Estate. Calliope gently held the fiddle to her chin. Then

she drew a ghostly bow across the strings. A haunting melody of mismatched notes echoed throughout the basement of Sleepy Hollow Elementary. Cocomo pointed her whiskers toward the ceiling and *meowed* along with the music.

"I think her cat likes the sound of the fiddle," Cassidy said.

Huxley, on the other hand, did not like the sound. He covered his ears with his paws and whined.

"At least things can't get much worse," Nina said, trying to sound cheerful as she flung a mashed banana into the trash.

But Nina was wrong — very wrong. Because just then, Edgar jumped up so high, his head got stuck in the ceiling. "I have an idea!" he hollered. "A wonderful, brilliant idea!"

9
Old-time Band

"We could form our own ghost band!" Edgar suggested. "It could be like the ones we had at the barn raisings. Remember how Uncle Theodore played music with his friends and we all danced?" Becky squealed, and Ozzy did a little jig on Mr. Morton's desk.

"Noooo," Sadie wailed. "I never learned to plaaayyyy muuuusiiic." Tears the size of marbles rolled down Sadie's cheeks and dribbled off her chin. The tears plopped on the floor by her feet and formed a huge green-tinted puddle.

"Don't worry," Becky told her. "We'll teach you."

Jeff ran between the ghosts. "No, you can't do that."

Swirls of green floated all around Jeff

as the ghosts disappeared. Ghostly laughter filled the air. "Oh, but we can," Calliope said. "And we will."

Jeff, Nina, and Cassidy grabbed their backpacks and started walking home. "It was bad enough when Calliope played the fiddle and sang," Nina said. "If they all play instruments, the noise will make me bonkers."

Jeff nodded. "They ruined my audition for the play."

"Don't worry," Cassidy said. "Calliope has her fiddle, but none of the other ghosts have instruments. What could they possibly do?"

The kids found out early the next morning when they saw a ghostly sign etched in the dirt on the window, which read, o⅃⅃y and the howlers.

Jeff, Nina, and Cassidy were the first kids in the classroom, except for the ghosts. "I can't believe it!" Nina said.

Jeff couldn't help grinning. After all, the ghosts were very resourceful. Ozzy banged on the bottom of a mop bucket. Nate played spoons that he snitched from left-behind lunchboxes. Becky and Edgar tapped pencils together while Sadie sang. Calliope played the fiddle and Cocomo howled.

Poor Huxley looked as upset as the kids. He had his head buried under his paws.

Nina tried to pet Huxley, but her hand kept going through his body. "What are we going to do now?" Nina asked her friends.

"We'll just have to use our acting skills to pretend like they aren't here," Jeff said.

Cassidy sighed. The band *thumped* and *bumped* and *screeched*. The song sounded a bit like "Oh My Darling Clementine." Ignoring them would definitely not be easy.

The kids tried. When Mr. Morton talked about the seven times table, the kids glued their eyes to him. During

spelling and reading, Jeff couldn't help tapping his foot under his desk. Every once in a while, Nina found herself humming along to the old songs the ghosts were singing. Cassidy almost clapped when the ghosts finally decided to take a break.

"Now," said Mr. Morton, "let's finish our play tryouts." Nina read for the part of Mama, and lots of kids tried to be little Arliss, since he was the funny one in the story.

After the tryouts, Mr. Morton split the class into two groups. One group had to choose the best parts from the book they were reading and make them into a play script. The other group designed props and the set for the play. Jeff, Nina, and Cassidy were chosen to write the script.

"I wanted to write the play on my own," Jeff said. "I even have a head start."

"I wanted to have peace and quiet,"

Cassidy said. "Those ghosts are driving me crazy with their music."

"Shh," Nina said. "Mr. Morton is announcing who gets to be the lead in the play."

Jeff held his breath and crossed his fingers as Mr. Morton held up the list of parts.

10
Cassidy's Plan

"I can't believe Andrew gets to be the star of *my* play," Jeff complained the next morning on the way to school. "I wanted to be Travis. Instead I have to be Pa."

"*Your* play?" Cassidy said. "I tried out for the lead, and I ended up being a dog!"

Nina patted Cassidy on the back. "The dog is the most important character," Nina pointed out.

Cassidy looked at Nina and growled.

"It's not fair," Jeff said. "Andrew doesn't even care about the play."

Nina stepped carefully to avoid a big crack in the sidewalk. "It doesn't matter who gets to be Travis. I have a terrible feeling the ghosts are going to ruin the play, anyway."

Cassidy nodded. "All that old-fashioned

music and banging gave me a really bad headache yesterday," she said. "But I have a plan."

"We could break all their instruments into little pieces," Jeff suggested.

"No," Cassidy said. "I'm talking about a real solution to our extra-ghost problem. All we have to do is take the fiddle and dish back to the Blackburn Estate where they belong."

Nina nodded. "That might work.

Calliope and her cat will have to leave with them."

"That's it!" Jeff yelled. "Then the other ghosts will forget about putting together a band, and things can get back to normal."

"It's too bad about Calliope," Nina said. "I bet she was lonely at the Blackburn Estate."

"Lonely!" Jeff snapped. "There are probably a million ghosts in that haunted house."

"We have to do this now," Cassidy told her friends, "before the ghosts totally ruin our play."

"But we have to go to school," Nina pointed out.

"School will just have to wait," Cassidy told her.

The kids quietly tiptoed down the back steps into their basement classroom. The lights were still off in the room, which meant Mr. Morton wasn't in school yet.

Thankfully, when they eased into the classroom, the ghosts weren't anywhere to be seen — or heard.

"Do you think ghosts sleep?" Nina whispered.

Cassidy shrugged. "Let's just get the fiddle and dish. Hurry!"

Jeff quietly scooted Mr. Morton's chair beside the shelf. He stood on the chair and grabbed the ghostly items. "Got them!" Jeff said.

But as soon as Jeff touched the fiddle and dish, the early morning calm was shattered. The lights flashed on and off.

The shades snapped up and down. Art supplies flew around the room. Chalk zipped through the air.

Nina screamed. "Ahhh! It's a ghost attack!"

11
Ghost Storm

The air in their classroom seemed to fill with storm clouds. It boiled and swirled until it took the shapes of Ozzy and his ghostly crew. This time, they didn't look friendly. Ozzy grew nine feet tall and glared down at the three kids.

"Give them back!" Ozzy howled, causing a wind that made pictures sway and papers fly off desks.

Jeff's face turned a sickly shade of green. Nina covered her eyes with her hands. Cassidy swallowed, but she didn't run or hide. She grabbed the fiddle and the tiny dish from Jeff. Then she faced Ozzy. "Never!" she said. "We're taking Calliope and Cocomo back where they belong."

Calliope floated helplessly above the

fiddle with Cocomo cradled in her arms. "We don't want to go," she cried softly. "We want to sing, sing, sing! Play, play, play!"

"That's exactly why you have to go home," Cassidy said. She turned her back on Ozzy and headed toward the door. "Let's go," she yelled to Jeff and Nina. But the three didn't get very far.

Ozzy, Nate, Edgar, Becky, and Sadie surrounded them. The ghosts filled their cheeks with air and blew hard. Nina, Jeff, and Cassidy were caught in a fierce whirlwind. Desks were smashed against the wall. Chairs tumbled. Cassidy, Jeff, and Nina held onto each other to keep from being blown away.

The harder the ghosts blew, the harder

it was for the three friends to make their way to the door. But they never gave up. Together, they pulled themselves along the walls until they reached the door. Cassidy threw open the door that led to the playground.

Calliope and Cocomo had no choice. They had to leave the basement. Halfway up the steps, Cassidy heard something so terrible, she couldn't move.

"What is it?" Nina asked.

"Whatever it is, it's hurting my ears," Jeff said.

Cassidy cautiously peeked back in the classroom. The ghosts were no longer the size of giants. They had collapsed on the floor like wasted balloons. Sadie was crying. Edgar was ripping pages from his journal. Becky pounded her little fists on the floor and screamed, "No, no, no!" Her fists sank into the floorboards with each word.

Together, the ghosts made a noise worse than anything the kids had heard in their lives — worse than the sound of the ghost band.

"No, no, no," Becky bawled.

"Bring them back," Nate yelled.

"No fair!" Ozzy added.

"It's so saaaaaaaad," Sadie sobbed.

"We'll never forget this," Edgar said. "And we won't let you forget it, either!"

Even Huxley whined because Cocomo was gone.

"This is worse than ever," Nina said. "They'll never leave us alone. What are we going to do now?"

12
Success

Cassidy stood at the classroom door. The furniture had all been blown to one side of the floor. The ghosts were scattered in the middle of the room. Mr. Morton was bound to walk in any minute. Cassidy had to do something, and she had to do it fast.

"Calliope and Cocomo belong at the Blackburn Estate," Cassidy told the ghosts. She tried to reason with them, but she didn't sound as sure as before. "Our classroom is no place for her music."

"This room is our home," Ozzy pointed out. "We can play music if we want."

"Your music is ruining our play," Jeff sputtered.

Ozzy laughed so hard he bounced up

and down. He bounced so high, his head smashed into the ceiling.

"What's so funny?" Jeff asked.

Edgar cleared his throat. "Actually, your class is ruining the play," he said. "You don't know what it was really like back in our times. Your script has so many mistakes."

"Mistakes?" Jeff said. "How can my script be wrong?"

"Well," Becky said, her hands on her

hips. "All you let the girls do is stitch and bake. We did lots of other things."

"And in the scene before the bull-fight, you have the characters listen-ing to some contraption called a radio," Ozzy said. "We don't even know what a radio is."

Jeff's ears turned red. He looked like he was ready to explode. Nina inter-rupted before Jeff blew his top. "Why don't you help us?" she asked the ghosts. "That way our play will be good — and correct!"

"That's it!" Cassidy said. "If you help us with the play, we won't bring Calliope and Cocomo back to the Blackburn Estate. For now."

The ghosts agreed. For the rest of the week, the kids listened to the ghosts and made changes to the script. Then, Calliope taught them songs that were sung in the 1800s.

Instead of singing their own songs on the day of the play, Ozzy and the

Howlers sang backup to Jeff and the rest of the cast. Of course, nobody but Jeff, Nina, and Cassidy could hear them. Although some kids were amazed that it sounded like a fiddle was playing along with them. But that was okay. With a little help from their ghost friends, the play was a great success.

Jeff had to admit that even though he wasn't the star, he liked being Pa, and Andrew was pretty good as Travis. Nina

made a great Ma, and everyone laughed when she grabbed little Arliss' ear and promised to switch him if he didn't quit swimming naked in the drinking water.

Cassidy was quite the hit as Old Yeller. Her grandfather had helped her make dog ears out of felt. Even Carla and Darla's little brother cheered for Cassidy, and Mr. Morton absolutely beamed.

"I'm glad we didn't make Calliope and Cocomo go back to the Blackburn Estate," Nina said after the rest of their classmates had left for the day. Cassidy, Nina, and Jeff were packing up to go home.

"Making a compromise was the best idea after all," Jeff said. "Working together made our play a success."

Cassidy turned out the light and closed the door to their empty classroom. As soon as she did, the three kids heard a high-pitched sound coming from inside their basement room.

"What is it?" Nina asked.

The kids held their breath so they could hear. It was a voice singing a song, but this wasn't a song from the 1800s. It was a brand-new song.

> *"Friends I haven't known for long,*
> *Make me sing a happy song."*

"It's Calliope," Jeff said with a grin, "and she's singing a song about us!"

"Maybe now it won't be so bad sharing our room with a bunch of ghosts," Cassidy said hopefully.

Just then, Cassidy heard Ozzy's voice. He was changing the words to Calliope's song, and the new words weren't very nice at all.

> *"Some new friends are a pain in the pants,*
> *So now that they're gone, I'll do a little dance!"*

Becky started laughing, but Sadie wailed, "Nooooooo!"

Cocomo *yowled* and Huxley *howled.* Something crashed to the floor, and from the sound of it, it was something big. Very big.

"And then again," Cassidy said, "I could be wrong. Ghost wrong!"

Ready for more spooky fun?
Then take a sneak peek at the next

Ghostville Elementary™

#6 Happy Boo-Day to You!

"Happy birthday to me," Nina sang. "Happy birthday to me."

It was the evening of Nina's sleepover party, and she was in her family's big sunny kitchen pouring lemonade. All of the girls from her class were downstairs in the basement. The fun had already begun. Nina just knew this would be the perfect birthday party.

When she picked up the tray filled with glasses and turned for the steps, her foot caught on the edge of a chair. Nina stumbled. The ice in the glasses clinked. The tray teetered in her grasp. Nina was sure the lemonade was going to spill everywhere, but at the last minute the tray seemed to right itself and Nina caught her balance.

"Whew," she said to herself. "That was a close call."

Suddenly, the tiny heart hanging at her throat felt like an ice cube and goose bumps scattered up her arms. Nina shivered and carried the tray of lemonade to her basement. She didn't spill one drop, even when she passed the glasses out to the girls.

"Let's play a game," Cassidy said after she drank a big gulp of lemonade.

"How about . . ." Carla said slowly

". . . pin the tail on the donkey?" Darla, her twin sister, suggested.

Cassidy nodded. It was a silly game, but who cared?

Everyone laughed when Carla pinned the tail on the donkey's nose. Darla ended up putting the tail on the donkey's ear.

Cassidy was sure she was heading to the right end of the donkey. When she pulled off the blindfold and saw the tail on the donkey's foot, she couldn't believe it. "You moved the poster," she yelled out. "I know I had it right."

A girl named Barbara shook her head. "No one touched that poster."

Barbara did even worse. Her tail wound up taped to the wall.

When Nina was blindfolded and twirled three times, she headed in the wrong direction. It looked like she was going to pin the tail on the couch. Carla giggled. Darla snickered. A few of the girls laughed out loud. Nina paused, and her free hand lifted the cold heart necklace away from her skin.

Suddenly, Nina swirled as if she had been turned by invisible hands. Her outstretched hand reached the paper tail toward the donkey's ears. Slowly, her arm moved along the poster until it hovered right where the tail needed to go. No one could believe it when Nina got the tail in exactly the right place.

"Have you been practicing?" Barbara teased. "That was like magic."

"Or maybe," Cassidy whispered, "it was a ghost . . ."

About the Authors

Marcia Thornton Jones and Debbie Dadey got into the *spirit* of writing when they worked together at the same school in Lexington, Kentucky. Since then, Debbie has *haunted* several states. She currently *haunts* Ft. Collins, CO, with her three children, two dogs, and husband. Marcia remains in Lexington, KY, where she lives with her husband and two cats. Debbie and Marcia have fun with spooky stories. They have scared themselves silly with *The Adventures of the Bailey School Kids* and *The Bailey City Monsters* series.

MORE SERIES YOU'LL LOVE

A JIGSAW JONES MYSTERY ™

Jigsaw and his partner, Mila, know that mysteries are like jigsaw puzzles— you've got to look at all the pieces to solve the case!

THE SECRETS -OF- DROON

Under the stairs a magical world awaits you.

Hey L'il D!

L'il Dobber has two things with him at all times—his basketball and his friends. Together, they are a great team. And they are always looking for adventure and fun—on and off the b'ball court!

www.scholastic.com/kids

LITTLE APPLE

LAPLT